T0377746

JUNIOR
BIOGRAPHIES

TAYLOR SWIFT

SINGER AND SONGWRITER

Enslow Publishing
101 W. 23rd Street
Suite 240
New York, NY 10011
USA

enslow.com

Heather Moore Niver

WORDS TO KNOW

contract An agreement between an artist and a record company.

cover To perform songs written by another person.

executive A high-level businessperson.

inspire To move someone to do something.

karaoke A performance of singing to prerecorded music.

nomination The suggestion that someone should be given an award or a position.

pop Short for, or related to, popular music.

record label A record company.

trivialize To make something seem less important.

CONTENTS

Taylor Swift

CHAPTER 1

A Musician's Childhood

On December 13, 1989, the music world was changed forever. Taylor Alison Swift was born in Reading, Pennsylvania. Her parents were Scott Kingsley and Andrea Swift. They both worked in banking. Taylor's grandmother, on the other hand, was an opera singer. Taylor also has a younger brother named Austin.

Growing Up

Taylor grew up in the country on a Christmas tree farm. "I had the most magical childhood, running free and going anywhere I wanted to in my head," she says. She loved horses and singing along to Disney movie songs.

When she was just a fourth grader, Taylor won a national poetry contest.

Taylor poses with her parents, Andrea and Scott Swift. They encouraged her to follow her dream to become a musician.

UNSTOPPABLE!

When Taylor was only nine, she started to show interest in music. She was **inspired** by country star Shania Twain. By the time she was ten, Taylor competed in public. She took part in **karaoke**

Taylor Says:

"Someday, when you get where you're going, you will look around and you will know—it was you, and the people who love you, who put you there. And that will be the greatest feeling in the world."

contests. "I sang every single week for a year and a half until I won," she admitted. The prize was that she got to be the opening act for country megastar Charlie Daniels!

By age twelve, Taylor was learning her way around a guitar. Soon she was even writing songs. Taylor remembers, "When I picked up the guitar, I could not stop."

Country singer Shania Twain was one of Taylor's inspirations when she was a girl.

CHAPTER 2
SWIFT RISES SWIFTLY

Recording company RCA offered Taylor a record deal when she was just thirteen years old. Clearly, Taylor was going to have a musical life. So her parents decided to move to Nashville, Tennessee. (The city is known as Music City, USA.) Taylor was homeschooled, and she finished her junior and senior years of high school in just twelve months—with straight As!

A NEW LABEL

Scott Borchetta was a record **executive**. He was about to start his own **record label**—Big Machine Records—when he first saw Taylor perform. She wowed him with her

> Taylor Says:
> **"Never believe anyone who tells you that you don't deserve what you want."**

In 2006, Taylor first hit it big in Nashville, Tennessee.

Taylor attends the fiftieth annual Grammy Awards, where she was nominated for Best New Artist.

songs at the Bluebird Coffee House. When RCA offered her another **contract**, she said no. Taylor wanted to record her own music, but RCA wanted her to **cover** other songs. So she signed with Borchetta instead.

FROM COUNTRY TO POP

Taylor's first album, *Taylor Swift*, hit the airwaves in 2006. It had five Top 10 singles and earned a Best New Artist Grammy **nomination**. (She lost to Amy Winehouse.)

Taylor worked hard on her second (*Fearless*) and third

Taylor performs at the MTV Video Music Awards in 2010.

> If you hear a Taylor Swift song, she wrote it. She writes all her own music, sometimes with a cowriter.

(*Speak Now*) albums. Together they sold twelve million copies in the United States!

Taylor was a country singer. A few of her songs played on **pop** radio, though. Her fourth album, *Red,* included some pop tunes. Listeners loved songs like "We Are Never Ever Getting Back Together."

Taylor's album *1989* was a pop album. It could have been a huge flop, but Taylor listened to her heart. Wow, was it worth it! It sold 1.287 million copies in just the first week!

Taylor's music has often centered around her love life. "I love love," she says. "I love studying it and watching it. I love thinking about how we treat each other, and the crazy way that one person can feel one thing and another can feel totally different."

LOVE SONGS

Taylor's romances (and breakups) have often been in the public eye. They have also inspired her songs. She has written songs about boyfriends Joe Jonas, Taylor Lautner, Jake Gyllenhaal, John Mayer, Harry Styles, and Tom Hiddleston. She says, "I don't like it when headlines read 'Careful, Bro, She'll Write a Song About You,' because it **trivializes** my work."

Taylor dated musician John Mayer in 2010. She has written many songs about her former boyfriends.

Music is not Taylor's only interest! She enjoys watercolor painting in her free time.

STRONG SISTERHOOD

Taylor is not just a lovesick songwriter. These days, she is more interested in a different kind of love. She's focused on being a good role model, especially for girls. One important part of supporting girls is to encourage them to support one another. "I surround myself with smart, beautiful, passionate, driven, ambitious women," she says.

Taylor Swift and Selena Gomez became friends in 2008 when they met backstage at a Jonas Brothers concert.

Taylor Says:

"All I ever do is learn from my mistakes so I don't make the same ones again. Then I make new ones. I know people can change because it happens to me little by little every day."

Taylor has a tight group of girlfriends, including long-time friend Selena Gomez, called the Girl Squad. "Other women who are killing it should motivate you, thrill you, challenge you and inspire you."

17

CHAPTER 4
BEYOND THE GLAMOUR: GIVING

Taylor Swift is busy. She's almost always writing, recording, or performing her music. But Taylor is as generous as she is glamorous. Over the years, she has shown her giving spirit in many ways.

In 2016, Louisiana experienced serious damage from rains and flooding. Eleven people lost their lives. Taylor said, "The fact that so many people in Louisiana have been forced out of their own homes this week is heartbreaking." She then donated one million dollars to help the victims of the flooding.

A million dollars is a huge donation, but it's just one of many. In 2016, Taylor gave to hospitals, to food banks, and to Dolly Parton's telethon to help victims of

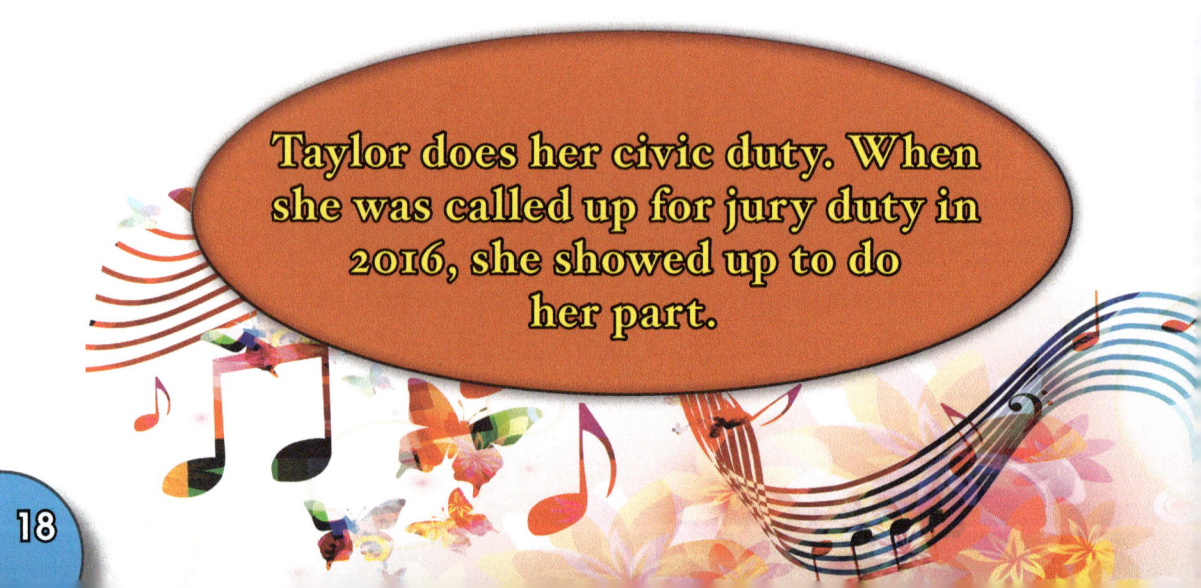

Taylor does her civic duty. When she was called up for jury duty in 2016, she showed up to do her part.

Taylor performs at a concert in British Columbia, Canada, as part of her *1989* World Tour Live.

Tennessee wildfires. And she once spent almost half an hour on Facetime, video chatting with a fan who had heart problems.

EVERYDAY KINDNESS

Taylor does not just show kindness in public ways. Once, during a magazine interview, a fan asked to have her picture taken with Taylor. It turned out to be the fan's

Taylor takes selfies with a crowd in 2012. The pop star makes sure to let fans know how important they are to her.

Taylor Says:

"I hope you know that who you are is who you choose to be, and that whispers behind your back don't define you. You are the only one who gets to decide what you will be remembered for."

birthday. When Taylor asked her how she was celebrating, the fan replied that she was going to an inexpensive restaurant. Without hesitating, Taylor reached into her purse and handed the girl some cash. "Go somewhere nice," she said.

And that's simply what Taylor is like. She may be a huge star, but she still takes time for her fans. And while her music continues to move in new directions, her kindness will never change.

TIMELINE

1989 Taylor Swift is born on December 13.

2004 Signs first record deal with RCA Records.

2005 Signs new record deal with Big Machine Records.

2006 *Taylor Swift* is released and sells more than five million copies in the United States.

2008 *Fearless* is released and goes on to become the top-selling US album in 2009.

2009 Taylor headlines her first concert tour.

2010 *Speak Now* goes to the top spot—number one—on the Billboard chart.

2011 Taylor releases a live album: *Speak Now–World Tour Live.*

2012 *Red* is released and sells one million copies in its first week.

2014 Pop album *1989* is released and sells 1.287 million copies in one week.

2016 Taylor wins three Grammy Awards at the 2016 ceremonies: Album of the Year, Best Pop Vocal Album, and Best Music Video for "Bad Blood."

LEARN MORE

BOOKS

Ryals, Lexi, and Erwin Madrid. *When I Grow Up: Taylor Swift.* New York, NY: Scholastic, 2015.

Schwartz, Heather E. *Taylor Swift.* Mankato, MN: Capstone Press, 2013.

Shaffer, Jody Jensen. *Taylor Swift.* Mankato, MN: Child's World, 2013.

WEBSITES

Billboard: Taylor Swift
www.billboard.com/artist/371422/taylor-swift
See how Taylor's songs did in the music charts and learn more about her through articles, photos, and a biography.

Official Taylor Swift Website
taylorswift.com
Check out the latest Taylor Swift news with photos, videos, and a community page for fans.

INDEX

Published in 2018 by Enslow Publishing, LLC.
101 W. 23rd Street, Suite 240, New York, NY 10011

Library of Congress Cataloging-in-Publication Data
Names: Niver, Heather Moore.
Title: Taylor Swift: singer and songwriter / Heather Moore Niver.
Description: New York: Enslow Publishing, 2018. | Series: Junior biographies
 | Includes bibliographical references and index. | Audience: Grades 3-5.
Identifiers: LCCN 2017018945| ISBN 9780766090590 (library bound) | ISBN
 9780766090576 (pbk.) | ISBN 9780766090583 (6 pack)
Subjects: LCSH: Swift, Taylor, 1989–Juvenile literature. | Country
 musicians–United States–Biography–Juvenile literature.
Classification: LCC ML3930.S989 N58 2018 | DDC 782.421642092 [B] –dc23
LC record available at https://lccn.loc.gov/2017018945

Printed in China

Photo Credits: Cover, p. 1 Mark Davis/Getty Images; pp. 2, 3, 22, 23, 24, back cover (curves graphic) Alena Kazlouskaya/Shutterstock.com; p. 4 Steve Granitz/WireImage/Getty Images; p. 6 Rick Diamond/ACMA2013/Getty Images; p. 7 Melissa Renwick/Getty Images; pp. 9, 20 © AP Images; p. 10 Lester Cohen/WireImage/Getty Images; p. 11 Kevin Mazur/WireImage/Getty Images; p. 14 Dimitrios Kambouris/Getty Images; p. 16 John Shearer/WireImage/Getty Images; p. 19 Jeff Vinnick/Getty Images; interior page bottoms (music notes) abstract/Shutterstock.com.